ABCDrive!

"Play With Me" Toys & Balloons

ABCDrive!

A CAR TRIP ALPHABET
by Naomi Howland

CLARION BOOKS · NEW YORK

Clarion Books
a Houghton Mifflin Company imprint
215 Park Avenue South, New York, NY 10003
Text and illustrations copyright © 1994 by Naomi Howland

Illustrations executed in acrylics and colored pencil
on Arches hot press paper
Text is set in 30-pt. Palatino
Book design by Carol Goldenberg
Printed in Singapore.

Library of Congress Cataloging-in-Publication Data
Howland, Naomi.
ABCDrive! : a car trip alphabet / by Naomi Howland.
p.   cm.
Summary: A car trip provides the opportunity to see or experience
things for every letter of the alphabet, from "ambulance" to "zoom."
ISBN 0-395-66414-4   PA ISBN 0-618-04034-X
[1. Automobiles—Fiction. 2. Alphabet.] I. Title. II. Title:
ABC drive!
PZ7.H847Ab   1994
[E]—dc20   93-11530
CIP
AC
TWP 10 9 8 7 6 5

For John

A ambulance

bus B

cement mixer

dump truck **D**

E

engine

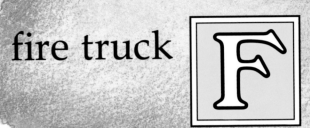

fire truck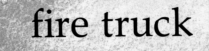

G garbage truck

headlights

I ice cream truck

jeep **J**

keys

limousine **L**

M motorcycles

no parking sign

O overpass

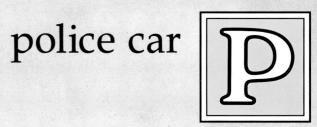

police car

Q quarter

red light R

S stop sign

traffic

U underpass

van V

wheels

xing (crossing)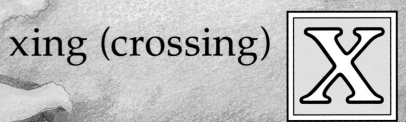

Y yield sign

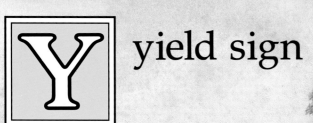

zoom